"My heart, O God, is steadfast;
I will sing and make music with all my soul.
Awake, harp and lyre! I will awaken the dawn."

Psalm 108:1–2

Under the Baobab Tree

WRITTEN BY

Julie Stiegemeyer

ILLUSTRATED BY

E.B. Lewis

ZONDERVAN.com/
AUTHORTRACKER
follow your favorite authors

ZONDERKIDZ

Under the Baobab Tree
Copyright © 2012 by Julie Stiegemeyer
Illustrations © 2012 by Earl B. Lewis

Requests for information should be addressed to:

Zondervan, *Grand Rapids, Michigan 49530*

Library of Congress Cataloging-in-Publication Data
Stiegemeyer, Julie.
   Under the baobab tree / by Julie Stiegemeyer.
       p.   cm.
   Summary: Moyo and his sister Japera hurry to the baobab tree in their
African village, wondering whether they will find peddlers, conversation
among the elders, storytellers, or perhaps something new.
   ISBN 978-0-310-72561-9 (hardcover)
   [1. Villages—Fiction. 2. Baobab—Fiction. 3. Brothers and sisters—
Fiction. 4. Christian life—Fiction. 5. Africa—Fiction.] I. Title.
PZ7.S855627Und 2012
[E]—dc23   2011030714

Editor: Barbara Herndon
Art direction and design: Kris Nelson

Printed in China

12 13 14 15 /LPC/ 21 20 19 18 17 16 15 14 13 12 11 10 9 8 7 6 5 4 3 2 1

About the Baobab Tree

The baobab tree, known as the tree of life, is commonly found in the hot and dry African savanna. It is called the tree of life because it has more uses than any other tree in the world, providing food, water, and shelter for both humans and animals. As the tree ages, it becomes hollow, supplying animals and humans with a place to live. Its leaves and fruit are filled with vitamins and nutrients. Elephants especially love its fruit! Much of the year, the tree is leafless, making it look as if it were upside down with its branches so bare that they look like roots. Along with its magnificent appearance and traits, the tree acts as a meeting place for the native African people to share stories and adventures with one another. It is highly regarded by the people as a mythical tree and is protected so that it will continue to provide them with remarkable gifts.

When the sun turns the morning sky to golden honey, a new day dawns, and Moyo steps from his straw-bound hut and begins his journey.

"Hurry, Japera," he calls to his sister. "Time to go!"

Moyo and Japera travel down the red, dusty road to the next village. There, they will gather under the baobab tree, the *tree of life*.

Moyo knows that some days the market wagon stops under the baobab tree. Villagers buy brightly colored cloth and heavy pots and pans.

But who will gather today under the baobab tree?

As the sun creeps above the horizon, Moyo gives thanks for the day as he watches clouds skim above the blue hills, hidden in shadow.

A weaverbird glances at Moyo and Japera as they pass by. Then the bird returns to building its basket-nest in the arms of an acacia tree.

Sometimes the elders gather under the baobab for long talks about the village and its people.

But who will gather today under the baobab tree?

Gazelle circle around a watering hole in the distance for a morning drink.
Water is drying up as everyone waits for God to send the big rains.

Moyo feels the morning sun in the red dirt under his bare feet. His short hair glistens in the heat of the day. Japera sings praises to her heavenly Father as she skips along beside Moyo.

Across the flat plain, Moyo sees a termite mound rising from the tall grass like a finger pointing to heaven.

Moyo knows that sometimes villagers come to share stories under the baobab tree. Tales of heroes and legends of the land are told under the branches of its gentle shade.

But who will gather today under the baobab tree?

Finally, Moyo and Japera race down the road as the village comes into view.
Dust billows behind the children as they hurry on.

Then, Moyo sees the giant baobab.
Ten children with arms wide open couldn't circle it. The old tree looks upside down; its gnarled branches, like roots, brush against the heavens.

But who will gather today under the baobab tree?

Moyo and Japera come to the end of their journey. They sit under the baobab, the *tree of life*. More and more people come to sit beside them.

Here there are no windows or doors.
No church bell or steeple.
No organ or flowers.

Just a cross and a Bible,
a pastor and songs,
voices and prayers.

And here everyone gathers ...

under the baobab tree.